Things
that
are

most

in the world

written by **Judi Barrett**

Things that are most in the world

illustrated by **John Nickle**

Atheneum Books for Young Readers

Atheneum
Books for Young Readers

An imprint of Simon & Schuster
Children's Publishing Division

1230 Avenue of the Americas
New York, New York 10020

Book design by Ann Bobco
The text of this book is set in Gill Sans Bold and Psycho Progressive.
The illustrations are rendered in acrylic paint.

First Edition
Printed in Hong Kong by South China Printing Co. (1988) Ltd.
10 9 8 7 6 5 4 3 2

Library of Congress Cataloging-in-Publication Data
Barrett, Judi.
 Things that are most in the world / by Judi Barrett ;
illustrated by John Nickle.—1st ed.
  p. cm.
  Summary: The reader who wants to know what are the quietest,
  silliest, smelliest, wiggliest things in the world finds imaginative
  answers to these and other questions about superlatives.
   ISBN 0-689-81333-3
   [1. Vocabulary.] I. Nickle, John, ill. II. Title.
   PZ7.B2752Th 1998
    [E]—dc21
     97-5155

To things that are the most, the least,
and everything in between
— J. B.

To Jana
"Who's the monkey?"
— J. N.

The

wiggliest

thing in the world

is

a snake ice-skating.

The silliest
thing in the world
is
a chicken
in a frog costume.

The

quietest

thing in the world

is

a worm

chewing peanut butter.

The

prickliest

thing in the world

is

the inside of a pincushion.

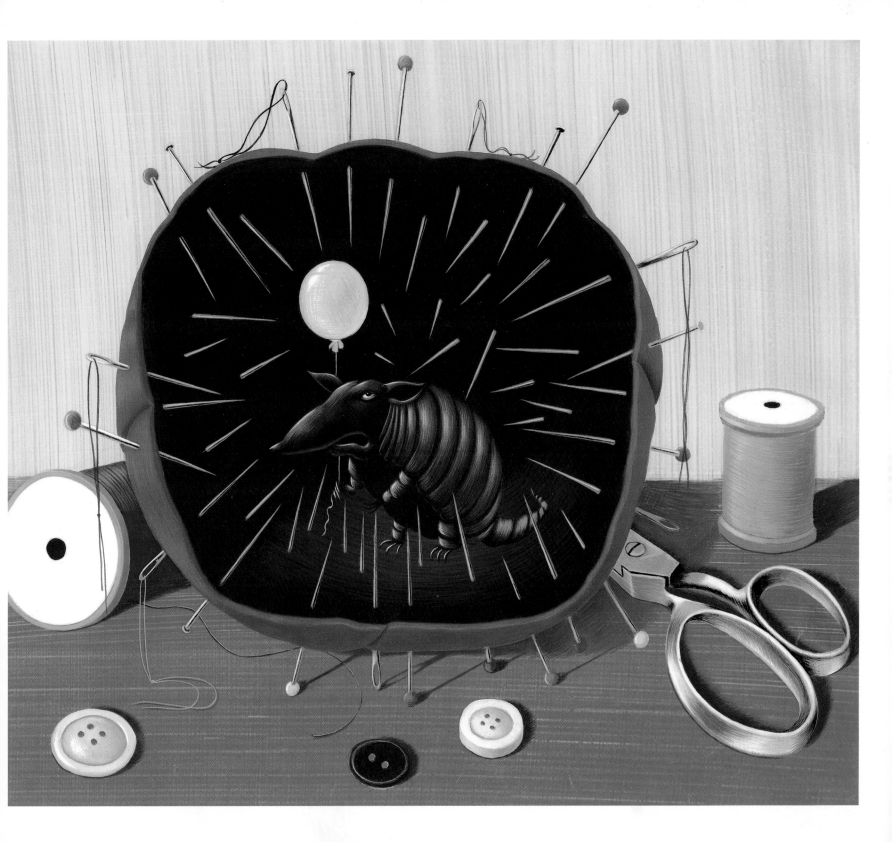

The hottest

thing in the world

is

a fire-breathing dragon

eating a pepperoni pizza.

The

oddest

thing in the world

is

an ant windsurfing

in a bowl of pea soup.

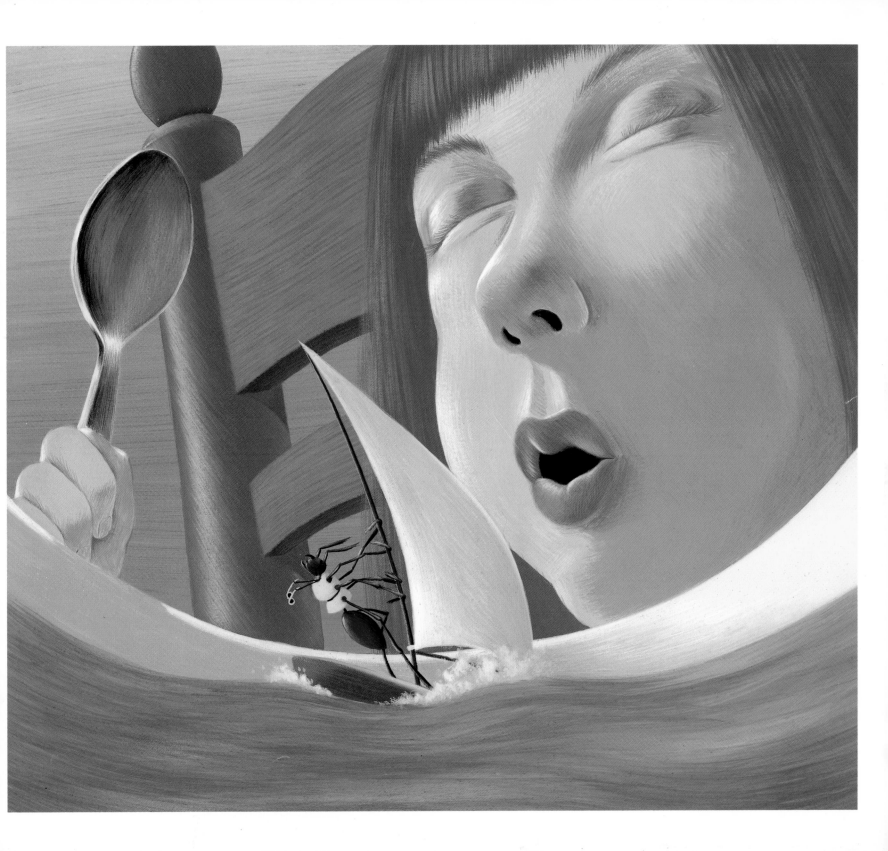

The

teensie-weensiest

thing in the world

is

a newborn flea.

The
longest
thing in the world
is
what you'd have
if you tied every single strand
of spaghetti together
end to end.

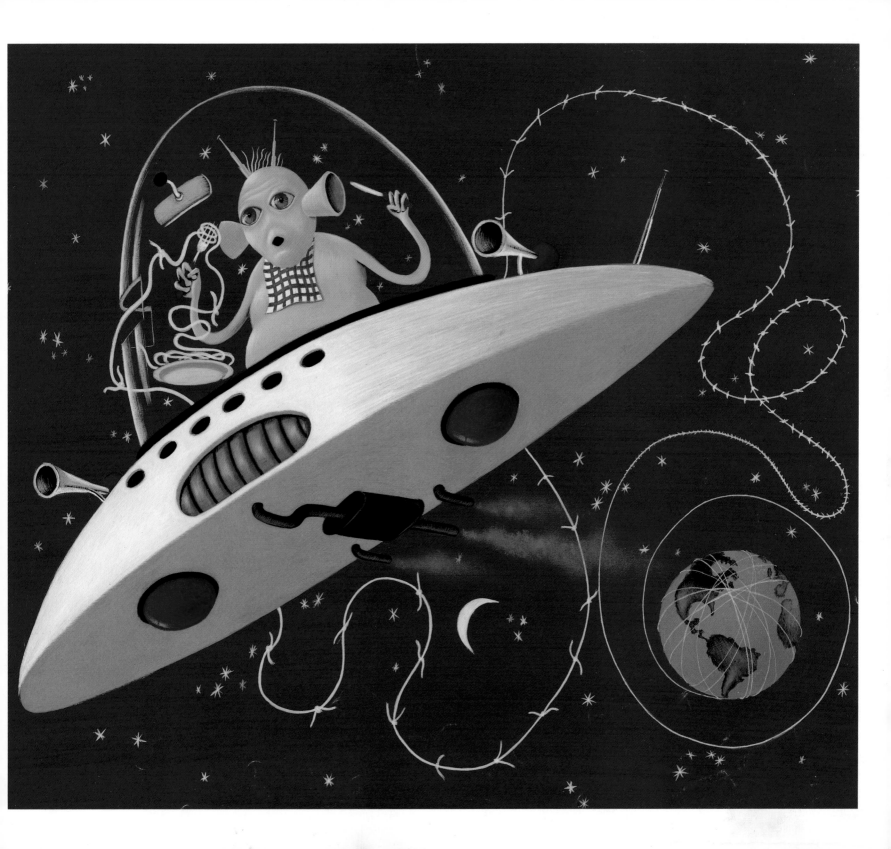

The

jumpiest

thing in the world

is

two thousand two hundred twenty-two toads

on a trampoline.

The
smelliest
thing in the world
is
a skunk convention.

The

stickiest

thing in the world

is

a 400,000-pound wad

of bubble gum.

The

heaviest

thing in the world

is

a Tyrannosaurus rex

weighing himself.

And the

highest

thing in the world

is

the very top of the sky.

The

_____est

thing in the world

is

_____●